Matilda's
Movie
Adventures

Lucy Dahl

VIKING

To Phoebe and Chloe

I would like to thank a handful of the many people who helped me, encouraged me and guided me, making this book possible: Danny DeVito, Rhea Perlman, Mara Wilson, Susie Wilson, Embeth Davitz, Pam Ferris, Michael Peyser, Josh Levinson, Peter Ward, Tracey Jones, John LaViolette, Kathy Rose, Sheila Morgan, and Regina Hayes.

Sadly, Susie Wilson died on April 26, 1996. She was the backbone of our team, a wonderful mother and a true friend. Those who found her never let her go . . . until we had to.

VIKING
Published by the Penguin Group
Penguin Books USA Inc., 375 Hudson Street, New York, New York 10014, U.S.A.
Penguin Books Ltd, 27 Wrights Lane, London W8 5TZ, England
Penguin Books Australia Ltd, Ringwood, Victoria, Australia
Penguin Books Canada Ltd, 10 Alcorn Avenue, Toronto, Ontario, Canada M4V 3B2
Penguin Books (N.Z.) Ltd, 182-190 Wairau Road, Auckland 10, New Zealand

Penguin Books Ltd, Registered Offices: Harmondsworth, Middlesex, England

First published in 1996 by Viking, a division of Penguin Books USA Inc.

1 3 5 7 9 10 8 6 4 2

I remember when I first heard of Matilda. It was 1987 and I was living abroad. My father didn't like the telephone very much, and so the majority of our communication was through letters. He wrote to me once a week. He didn't often mention his work, but this book was special!

"I'm working on a story about a clever little girl with beastly parents. When you come home next month, it should be finished, and you can read it."

I clearly remember reading *Matilda*. I read the manuscript from beginning to end in one sitting. I loved it!

"This is my favorite so far," I told him. He dedicated it to me.

Eight years later, I found myself in Los Angeles, California, working on *Matilda's Movie Adventures*! Any apprehension that I may have had quickly diminished as I came to know Danny DeVito and his passion for my father's work. I was quite obviously the rookie on the set, and nervous that I would get in the way, knock something over, and get kicked off for ignorance in film making. Even if that was so, and I'm sure, at times it was, I was welcomed into Danny's team, and led by the hand into the wonderful world of *Matilda*, the movie. There were many days when I wished that my father could be with me, not only to help me with this book, but to witness the love and care that was taken by an extraordinary team of people, led by an extraordinary man.   —L. D.

This is me,
MATILDA
WORMWOOD.
I am six
years old.

This is my family.

They call me **the mistake**.
They don't like me very much.
I don't like them either!

My father owns a second-hand car garage.
He lies about his cars and cheats people.

My mother plays *bingo* all day, every day!

My brother sucks up to my father,

and I do my best to stay out of their way.

I'm old enough to go to school, but my parents have forgotten how old I am. **I am six.** <u>They say I'm four</u>. So every day I either stay at home, or I scrub the floors of **Wormwood Motors.**

Sometimes, I get left at home alone. **I like that.**

I can do what I love to do most—**READ.**

I don't really know how I learned to read. It just happened.

I asked my father for a book when I was four.

He said, **"Why would you want to read, when you've got the television set?"**

One day I looked up "L" for library in the telephone book and ventured out to find it.

And my **whole life changed.**

I found my first friend, Mrs. Phelps, the librarian.

I felt for the first time ever that I *belonged* somewhere. **I read and I read and I read.**

It's easy to join a library.

You can take lots of books home.
And you can **disappear** into the world of
d r a g o n s
  and **lions** and **witches**
    and **chocolate factories**.
You can make **new friends**
    and go on a **new adventure** <u>whenever you want</u>.

And then it makes you want to write, and so I did.
I STARTED A SECRET DIARY.

MATILDA's Secret Diary

KEEP OUT!!

If anyone reads this, I will know.

So put my diary down
RIGHT NOW!

★ ★ August 10th ★ ★

It is a usual evening at home.
My parents and my brother are watching TV.
We ate TV dinners.
I asked Dad today if I could go to school.

He said, "No."

I'm lonely. I want some friends.
I want to play with other kids.
I wish I had parents who knew my age.

Thank goodness for my books—otherwise,
I might think my family is NORMAL!

Being a kid is hard.
Grown-ups can do whatever they WANT,
whenever they WANT.
They eat what they WANT,
they go to bed when they WANT,
they can shout at us when they WANT,
and we can't shout back.

"I'm smart. . . .
You're dumb.

I'm **big**. . . .
You're little.

I'm right. . . .
You're wrong.

AND THERE'S *NOTHING*

YOU CAN DO ABOUT IT."

oh, but there is . . . in fact
there are LOTS of things. . . .

★★ August 24th ★★

Today Dad was teaching me to use Super-Super Glue to stick a brand-new shiny bumper on a very old car and make it look new.

Mom pulled up in her flashy new car with a fistful of money. (She won the Bingo jackpot.) Dad's eyes almost popped out of his head. He is very greedy and loves money.

Sometimes I like to play little tricks on my parents. Never anything that can really hurt them, just a little tweak here and there.

Mom took us to a fancy restaurant.

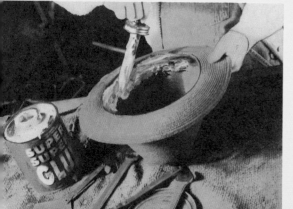

"Take your hat off, Harry."

"I can't. It won't come off."

"Don't be ridiculous. Take it off."

"It's stuck to my head!"

Mom had to cut it off with the kitchen scissors!

Now he looks like he had a fight with the lawn mower and lost!

(They have no idea it was me.)

I'm going to school!

The headmistress of Crunchem Hall School came to buy a car today, and Dad told me that I could go to her school.

Tomorrow!

I hope he didn't sell her a really rotten, stuck-together car. . . .

★★ september 2nd ★★

CROUCHED HALL

School
starts
today.

I was so excited,
I couldn't eat any breakfast.
Nobody noticed.

I **HOPE** the headmistress is nice.

"Grow up faster."

"Detention."

"Too blonde."

"Too curly."

"Sixty lines . . .
   I must obey Miss Trunchbull."

"Stomach in."

"Shoulders back."

"Feet together."

Miss Trunchbull
   is her name and she hates kids!

RULES OF CRUNCHEM HALL

1. NO talking
2. NO laughing
3. NO whispering
4. NO gum chewing
5. NO late homework
6. NO running in halls
7. NO pigtails
8. NO eating
9. NO coloring
10. NO praying
11. NO playing
12. NO daydreaming
13. NO FUN

Her rules are not to be broken!

Poor Amanda Thripp broke rule seven.

"Are you a PIG, Amanda?"

"No, Miss Trunchbull."

"What are those things hanging by your ears?

Pigtails?"

"B—b—but my mommy likes them."

"Then your mother is a PIG . . . and <u>you</u> are a PIGLET!"

"But—"

Never say "but"
or contradict The Trunchball.

My teacher is the nicest
grown-up I have ever met!
Her name is Miss Honey.

I think I'm going to like school.

I must stay out of the way
of that MISS TRUNCHBULL.

★★ September 8th ★★

I'm so happy!

I had a great day today playing
with my new school friends.

We caught newts in the stream.
They look like lizards.

Lavender took one home in a jar.

★★ September 13th ★★

Bruce Bogtrotter snuck into the school kitchen, and ate a slice of The Trunchbull's precious chocolate cake!!!!

Not the smartest thing to do!

The Trunchbull called an EMERGENCY ASSEMBLY and ordered Bruce to the stage.

A single slice of chocolate cake was placed in front of him.

I knew she was up to something horrible.

HE CHEWED. . . .
HE SWALLOWED. . . .
HE SMILED. . . .

There was <u>nothing</u> wrong with it!

Then Cookie appeared with a **G I A N T** chocolate cake.

"You will not leave the platform until you have consumed the <u>entire</u> confection." said The Trunchbull.

One mouthful . . . two . . . three . . . twenty-four . . . thirty-seven. He turned a peculiar shade of green, but he kept going and going and going. Mouthful after mouthful . . .

HE DID IT!

He ate the cake!

The whole thing!

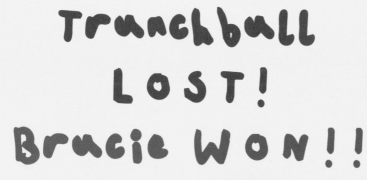

Trunchbull LOST! Bracie WON!!

The Trunchbull put me in The Chokey this morning because the car my father sold her broke down, and she blamed ME! A minute in there feels like an <u>hour</u>, and you wonder if it's day or <u>night</u> because you have been in there for SO LONG. The door is locked, and all you can see is spikes and broken glass. You can't move, because you'll get poked, and it smells like a public toilet!

Miss Honey came and rescued me. Then something incredible happened. . . .

When we got back to class, I noticed
Lavender's newt squirming around in The
Trunchbull's water glass! The Trunchbull
was busy
dangling
Nigel Hicks
upside down
because he
got an
answer
wrong.

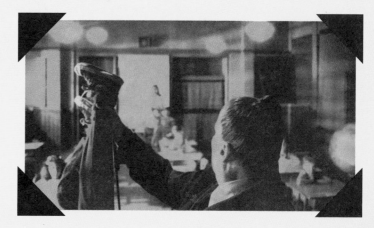

She reached for her glass of water. . . .

oh, no. . . .

Suddenly, the whole room
E X P L O D E D !

Her face got all RED
and she started screaming,

"A snake! A snake!"

"Actually, it's a newt," I explained.

I shouldn't have said
anything, because then
The Trunchbull turned on ME.

The more I tried to defend myself,
the more she shouted.

"I'm **big** and
you're small.
I'm right and
you're wrong.

AND THERE'S
NOTHING
YOU CAN DO
ABOUT IT."

I hate The Trunchbull.
My eyes began to burn.
All I wanted at that moment
was to tip the glass onto her.
I STARED at the glass.
It began to wobble. . . .

"Tip it. . . . Tip it. . . . Tip it!

Tip it. . . . Tip it. . . . Tip it!"

Then suddenly . . .

CRASH!

The glass fell, and the newt flew into the air and landed SMACK on The Trunchbull's enormous bosom! She shrieked.

Did I really do that? And if I did, HOW did I do it?

After school today, Miss Honey invited me to her cottage. It is very cozy but she has no electricity or hot water.

I didn't know that Miss Honey was so POOR.

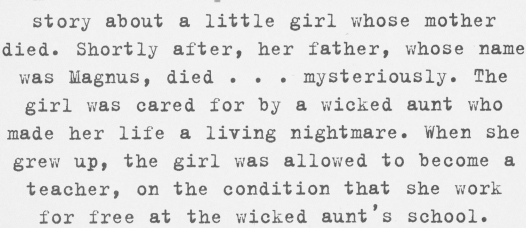

She told me a story about a little girl whose mother died. Shortly after, her father, whose name was Magnus, died . . . mysteriously. The girl was cared for by a wicked aunt who made her life a living nightmare. When she grew up, the girl was allowed to become a teacher, on the condition that she work for free at the wicked aunt's school.

Suddenly it all made sense!
I realized that the little girl
was Miss Honey, and . . .

oh no — that means . . .

THE TRUNCHBULL

is Miss Honey's aunt!

Miss Honey was given a tiny allowance,
and with that, she rented a cottage to
live in and was free! She left so quickly
that all of her treasures were left behind,
and her aunt Trunchbull would not allow her
back into the house to get them.

After school today, Miss Honey and I walked over to Miss Trunchbull's house. We watched her leave for the gym. Then we slipped into the house.

Miss Honey showed me all of her favorite things.

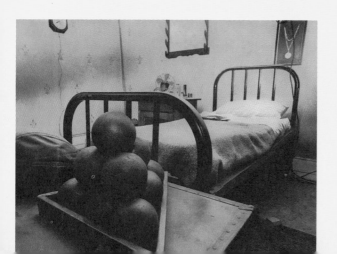

The Trunchbull's bedroom was H O R R I B L E !

And then suddenly, SHE WAS BACK! We were trapped in the house!

"**Who** is in my house?"

We hid behind doors, ran down stairways, and I even shimmied up under a table. If The Trunch had caught us, she would have TORTURED us.

We were lucky. We escaped.

Miss Honey made me promise never to go into the house again.

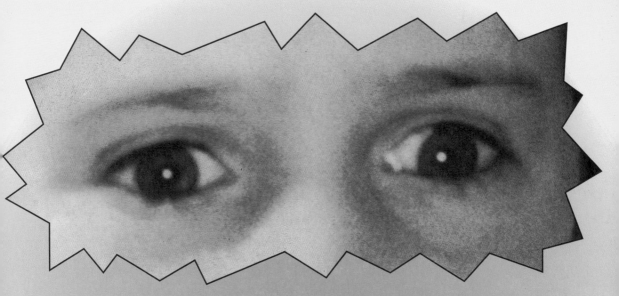

I have not written for a couple of days.
I have been really busy practicing my powers.

I've discovered that they work best when I'm angry.

There is one thing I want to do
more than anything.

I think tomorrow
will be the big night!

Look out you old Trunchbull!

★★ october 13th, A.M. ★★

I woke up early this morning.
TONIGHT IS THE NIGHT.
I didn't eat any breakfast.
N o b o d y   n o t i c e d !

(I must try to act normal
at school today.)

★★ october 13th, P.M. ★★

It's a really dark night.
My parents and Michael are glued
to the television.

That's GOOD—
they won't
notice
that
I'm gone.

If I don't make it back alive, and
anyone finds this diary, I would like
Miss Honey to have Wanda (my doll),
and my books that Mrs. phelps gave me.

I crept over to The Trunchbull's property. I couldn't go into the house, because I had promised Miss Honey that I would never do that again.
I climbed up onto the garage roof and powered Miss Honey's doll out of the window and safely into my arms.

MISSION ACCOMPLISHED!

I crept around the side of the house. I peeked inside. There was The Trunchbull . . . SHARPENING HER JAVELIN!
I wanted to get a chocolate for Miss Honey.
I powered open the windows. She closed them. Then I did it again.
SHE DIDN'T LIKE THAT.

I scared her!

Flashing lights!
Flying portraits!
Banging doors!

I opened all the windows and powered out two scrumptious chocolates. One for Miss Honey, and one for me! **MISSION COMPLETED!**

Always stop while you're ahead.

When I got home, everyone was still watching **TV.**

I've lost my red ribbon. I'll have to get another one tomorrow.

This day was the most triumphant day in history. First, when I arrived at school, I gave Miss Honey her doll and a chocolate. The bell rang and I went into class.

Then the door flew open! The Trunchbull marched in, with my red ribbon in her hand!

I was caught.
I had no alibi.
There was no way out.
THEN I HAD AN IDEA.

Everyone is scared of something, usually of having their deepest, darkest secrets revealed.

MY EYES BEGAN TO BURN AGAIN. I stared really hard at the blackboard, and the chalk began to write.

Agatha,
Thi

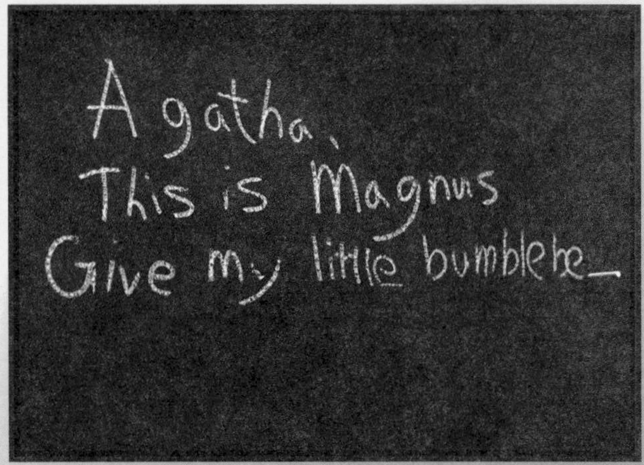

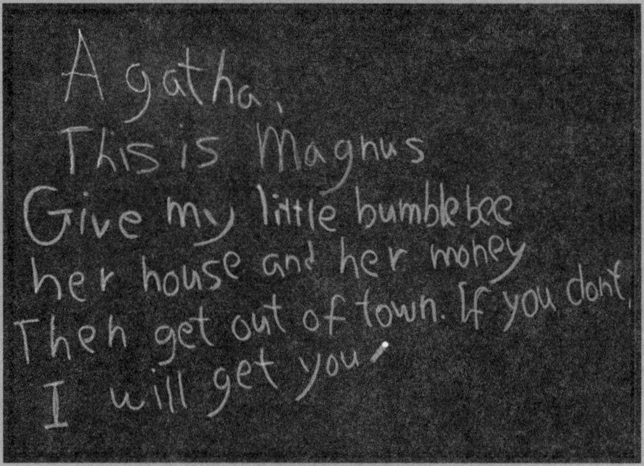

Agatha,
This is Magnus
Give my little bumblebe_

Agatha,
This is Magnus
Give my little bumblebee
her house and her money
Then get out of town. If you dont,
I will get you.

The whole
class was
reading my
message
OUT LOUD.

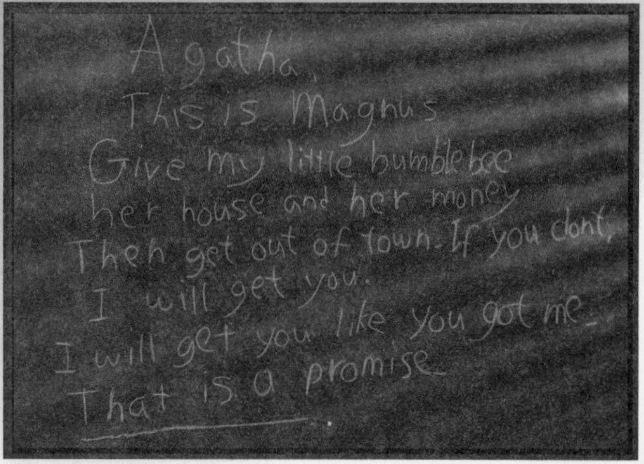

Agatha,
This is Magnus
Give my little bumblebee
her house and her money
Then get out of town. If you dont,
I will get you.
I will get you like you got me.
That is a promise.

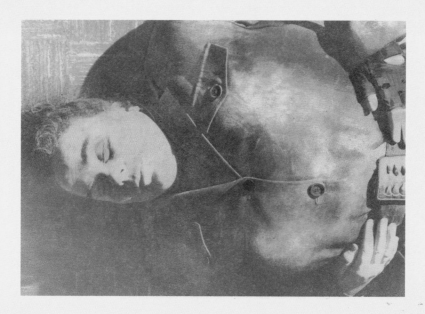

The Trunchball
FAINTED!

She stumbled to her feet . . .
fell onto the globe . . .
ZOOMED around and around . . .

FASTER AND FASTER.

Then she went for Lavender.
I POWERED her up to safety.

The Trunchbull was
DEFEATED!

The whole
school chased
her away.

And that
was the last
we EVER
saw of her.

★★ october 28th ★★

It has been two weeks since we got rid
of The Trunchbull.
Miss Honey is the new headmistress.

I think we should rename the school
H O N E Y   H A L L.
Miss Honey is living in her house once again.
I usually go and play after school on her swing,
or read books. She has a wonderful library.

My parents don't notice
that I'm not home very often.

★★ November 1st ★★

I have a new home.

COUNTY COURT RELINQUISHMENT DOCUMENT
PARENTS' RELEASE OF CHILD — ADOPTION

We **Harry and Zinnia Wormwood**

being the **parents**

of a **girl** child named **Matilda**

born the **8th** day of **August** A.D. 19 **88**

in the **United States** of **America**

and being solicitous that said child be cared for or placed in a suitable home by adoption or otherwise under the laws of this state, do hereby of our own free will and accord fully release and surrender said child

to **Jennifer Honey**

We are fully appraised of the fact that we need not execute this release unless we desire to do so of our free will and accord, but that once having executed this release, we thereby lose any and all rights in, to, and concerning this child forever.

In witness whereof, we do hereby set our hands and seal on

this **1st** day of **November** A.D. 19 **95**

Signed, sealed, and delivered: *Zinnia Wormwood*
Harry Wormwood

Today I was adopted by Jennifer Honey.

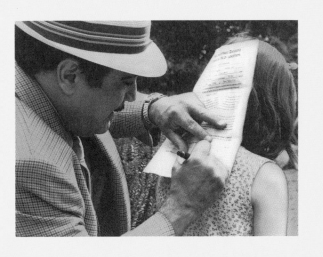

My parents
signed the
adoption
certificate

as they
R A C E D
off to the
airport

to escape
from the
FBI....

This is me,
Matilda HONEY.
I am seven
years old.

The end.

MATILDA'S TIPS
FOR SURVIVING SCHOOL

1. BIG does not mean SMART

2. BULLIES are BULLIES because
they are SCARED

3. NOBODY can MAKE you cry

4. Don't COMPETE — just know
the TRUTH

5. Never tell on your friends
(you won't have any if you do!)

6. When all else fails —
try sucking up!

7. Be BRAVE — don't let fear stop you

8. A punishment never lasts forever

9. READ — READ — READ

10. Stick with your friends

Mara's Diary

My name is **MARA WILSON**.
I am seven years old.
I live in Burbank, California.
I have a big family. . . .

Copyright © Nate Shapiro, 1995

Mom: She is my best friend and partner.

Dad: He is my friend, too. He is an engineer for television. He is very funny.

I have **three brothers** and **one sister**:

Danny, age sixteen. He talks all the time! He runs track, and likes people. He gets along with everybody.

Jonathan (we call him Jon), age fourteen. He likes to pole vault. His goal is nine feet. He fools around with computers. He knows a lot. In fact, he is our family encyclopedia.

Joel, age twelve. He helps me with the computer. He is the family detective. If anything is missing, he can find it!

I'm next, **Mara**, age seven.

Anna, age two. She is funny, cute, and sometimes stubborn.

THE BEGINNING

When I was six, I came home from school, and my mother gave me a movie script to read.

It was called <u>MATILDA</u>.

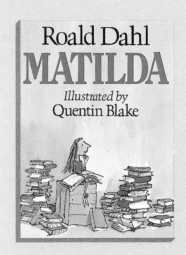

"Is it like the book?" I asked.

"I don't know," my mother answered. "Why don't you read it and find out?"

I went to my room and read the script. I was laughing out loud, and I called to my mother,

"It is just like the book. I love it!!!!"

Two weeks later, I met with the director, DANNY DeVITO, and read through parts of the script. The director is in charge of the actors. I knew that there were other kids auditioning for the part of Matilda. I was a little nervous, but I did my best, and tried not to get too excited about the movie, in case I wasn't chosen.

A week later, Mom told me that they wanted me! I WAS SO HAPPY.

<u>And that is how my Matilda adventure began</u>.

A month before we began filming, the serious work began. I was busy learning my lines and rehearsing with the other cast members.

The costume designer came to my house with three big racks of clothes for me to try. I looked best in green, but they decided that color had to be saved for Miss Trunchbull's costume. Miss Honey was in soft floral colors, so we chose blue for most of my wardrobe.

The makeup test was fun. Matilda needed dark circles under her eyes, to make her look sad and lonely. The makeup artist copied the face of her favorite childhood doll, who was called Pitiful Pearl, to give me a pale look. Every day my pink cheeks were covered over with stage makeup, and I was transformed into Matilda.

All actors have to wear stage makeup. It is like regular everyday makeup, but a little thicker. It stops the reflection of the lights from the camera.

As we got closer and closer to the shooting day, I was more and more excited. . . .

MAY 1995
DAY ONE OF FILMING,
WORMWOOD MOTORS

I AM SICK. <u>I CAN'T BELIEVE IT</u>! I've waited and waited for this day to come, and I HAVE THE FLU!

My mom says it's okay, Matilda is supposed to look sad and miserable. I'm not sad but I don't feel good at all. I have a fever of 103°.

In between takes, I go to my trailer and rest.

DANNY DeVITO is the director. He also plays Matilda's father. We are doing the scene where he shouts at me and calls me dumb and says I'm wrong.

Because in real life he is such a nice man, I have a problem keeping a straight face. I keep wanting to smile at him when he is shouting!

CAFE LE RITZ

Today is a fun day. We are at Café le Ritz. I am still a little sick, but feeling much better. We are filming the scene where Matilda's dad's hat is stuck to his head, and Zinnia, her mom, is trying to pull it off.

Zinnia is played by RHEA PERLMAN. She is DANNY DeVITO's wife in real life. They are **nothing** like the Wormwoods. I have been to their house. They eat delicious food, and there is a whole library full of books. They have three kids, two girls and a boy. They love them all. The kids have lots of animals.

At Café le Ritz, I have to eat a raspberry tart. I am not a big fan of raspberries, so they put whipped cream on top. Now I only have to eat the cream. When a film is being made, each scene is filmed again and again until it's perfect. So I had to eat about fifteen spoonfuls of whipped cream. It was good at first, but after the tenth mouthful I WAS SICK OF IT!

When the cakes started flying around, Michael (my brother in the film) got chocolate mousse all over his face. That was funny. The mousse was blown through a hidden air gun under the table.

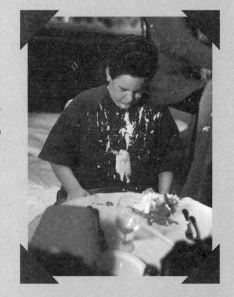

DANNY DeVITO REALLY DID CRASH INTO THE CAKE TABLE!

SCHOOL

I am working every day, so I can't go to school. I have a teacher here. Between scenes, we go to a small trailer nearby where it is quiet, and I keep up with my schoolwork. <u>I love reading, just like Matilda does</u>. My teacher is nice.

But sometimes I miss my school.

When there are other kids working on the film, I study with them, too. Today, I met "little Matilda," the girl who plays Matilda when she is younger. Her name is Sarah. She is five years old. She is really sweet and very smart. I think she looks a little like me, but not exactly.

THE CHOCOLATE CAKE

I feel really bad for Bruce Bogtrotter. I mean, fifteen spoonfuls of whipped cream is <u>NOTHING</u> compared to a WEEK of chocolate cake!

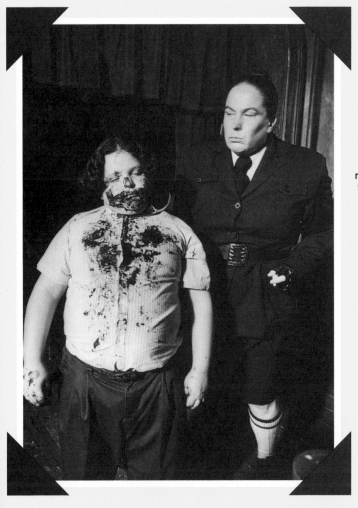

On the first day, I asked him if he liked chocolate cake.

"A little," he replied. That is really too bad!! <u>At first</u> the cake looked YUMMY. By the end of the week, I was tired of smelling it, and I asked Bruce how he was feeling. **"I'm sick of it,"** he answered.

I love chocolate, but that just might cure me FOREVER!

MISS HONEY

<u>I love working with Miss Honey</u>. Her real name is EMBETH DAVIDTZ. Today we are filming the scene where we are having tea. Normally, this would be a very serious acting day, because of all the lines I have to remember and the sadness of Miss Honey's story. But instead, it is like working with my BEST FRIEND.

We like to play tricks. At lunch,

Embeth put a single hair from her head on a clean plate. She added a little water. "Look!" she said to the assistant director. "There is a hair on my plate, and it's moving!" He looked closely, and when he was close enough, **Embeth hit the bottom of the plate and he got splattered with water!**

This morning, I brought Eleanor, my hamster, in to work with me so that I could show Embeth. (She loves animals.)

"I have a surprise for you!" I told her while we were in the makeup trailer.

"That's funny," she exclaimed, "I have a surprise for you, too."

She took me to her trailer, and as she opened the door, a bulldog puppy jumped out!

HE WAS THE CUTEST THING I HAD EVER SEEN.

She asked me to help her think of a name for him. Then I took her next door to my trailer to see my hamster. I named it after President Franklin D. Roosevelt's wife, Eleanor.

Embeth said, "Where's Franklin?"

"There isn't one." I replied.

"There is now. What a perfect name for my puppy! We will call him Frank for short."

THE TRUNCHBULL HOUSE CHASE

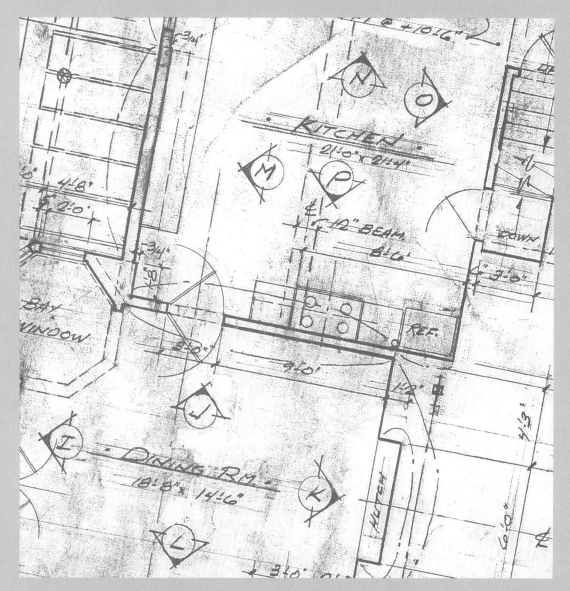

Miss Trunchbull's house was built just for this movie, <u>inside a studio</u>.

This is the floor plan.

THEY <u>BUILT</u> A REAL HOUSE!

Filming the chase was fun, because there were
stunts.* The actress who plays the Trunchbull, PAM
FERRIS, is very nice. She is an amazing actress, and
underneath all of the makeup and padding, she is a
really beautiful woman.

To prepare for the part of Miss Trunchbull, she had
to work with a professional trainer who taught her how
to throw the shot
put, the javelin—
and CHILDREN!

Pam also
did stunts, which
included jumping
over a banister!

But I was relieved to
see a real stunt woman
dressed as The Trunchbull
make the jump that was
twenty feet to the ground.
Although I think Pam could
have probably done it.

* Please don't try any stunts
at home. They're dangerous.

Today I got hoisted up under the table at The Trunchbull house. **THAT WAS <u>REALLY</u> FUN!**

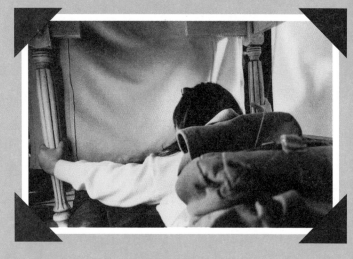

Another stunt I liked was climbing up onto the roof of The Trunchbull's house, with wind machines blowing me around! Everyone gets really nervous when I'm doing dangerous stuff, because if I fall and hurt myself, they will have to stop making the film, and that could be a big problem.

Even the newts used for The Trunchbull's water-glass scene were <u>stunt</u> newts.

Here is a letter from their owner to Emily, the person in charge of props.

10-2-95

Dear Emily,

I just wanted to thank you for your kindness and your professionalism. It is always refreshing to find intelligence and competence in "the business." I hope I will have the privilege of working with you again. On behalf of myself and the stunt newts, "Mr. Speaker," Wayne, and Sir Isaac (they should be in the credits), thank you.

Sincerely,

CRUNCHEM HALL EXTERIOR

Today is a really hot day, about 110°. The dress I am wearing is itchy in this heat.

PAM FERRIS (Miss Trunchbull) has to wear her wool suit, and underneath that, padding to make her look big. In between takes, she is connected to an air pipe, sort of like an air-conditioning vent, that goes up her skirt and underneath her padding. This keeps her somewhat cool.

We have a Sno-Kone machine, and tents are set up with water mist. We can go in there and cool off. Some people were given ice cold cloths to wipe their faces with, but the actors can't do that because it will ruin our makeup. We are only allowed lemon flavored Popsicles, because the orange and red ones color our lips and tongues. We also have to drink a lot of water so we don't get dehydrated.

AIR PIPE

THE TRUNCHBULL CHASE

Poor PAM FERRIS. Today, we were chasing her out of the school. It is still boiling hot, and she has to run away with all the kids throwing cake and candy, rolls of toilet paper, and all kinds of things at her! She never complains. <u>She is really a good sport!</u>

THE WHAMMY

When we first started this movie, Danny DeVito asked me how I wanted to express Matilda's powers through my eyes. I practiced lots of different things. Eventually I settled on a tilt of my head and a slight wink. THE WHAMMY.

Danny called it that. . . . I would be doing a scene and he would shout, "Give it the whammy." Something always happened! **I WISH I REALLY DID HAVE POWERS.** I would POWER my homework done. I'd POWER my room clean. If my mom was on the telephone and I wanted to ask her something, I would stare at the phone and it would hang up! If my brothers were annoying me, I'd POWER them too!

THE WORMWOOD HOUSE

This has been my favorite day of filming. It was the <u>dancing whammy</u> day.

At first, I didn't like dancing in front of all the crew, while they just stood there watching me, so DANNY DeVITO made <u>everyone</u> dance, <u>all day</u>. Whenever the music came on, whoever was on the set had to dance. It was really fun. Even my mom was dancing!

Danny would shout, "Whammy the cushion!"

I did. It started spinning. Then he would shout, "Whammy the lamp!" and it turned on.

"Whammy those cupboard doors!" and they started banging open and closed. I was dancing at the same time, and at one point, I almost believed I was making it all happen. IT WAS SO COOL!

The music was loud and <u>everything</u> I whammied started moving!

MY NEW FRIENDS

I really like my new friends. We love to play tricks on the adults.

Today we wrote notes on big pieces of paper, like:

KICK ME!!   **HUG ME!!**

KISS ME!!

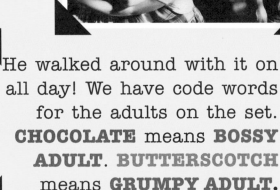

Then we stuck a note on the assistant director's back!

He walked around with it on all day! We have code words for the adults on the set. **CHOCOLATE** means **BOSSY ADULT**. **BUTTERSCOTCH** means **GRUMPY ADULT**. **APPLE PIE** means **VERY CRANKY ADULT**. The adults don't have any idea! They probably have been called worse names than **chocolate** and **apple pie** anyway.

Some days I work with lots of kids, but Shannon is with me every day. She is my photo double. She is fun to play with. We work almost the same hours. She wears the same clothes as me and looks just like me from behind.

AMANDA THRIPP'S FLIGHT

Amanda Thripp got thrown across the playground today. It was fun to watch. I was jealous. I wish I could be thrown; it looks like so much fun. She wasn't nervous at all. In fact, while they were attaching the wires to her, she was <u>reading a book</u>!

This is how they did it.

Although I didn't get the chance to fly, my mother and I did go up in the giant condor crane about seventy feet. THAT WAS <u>GREAT</u>.

THE CHOKEY

I was afraid of going into The Chokey, because I don't like small dark spaces (especially ones with spikes and dripping water). The Trunchbull is going to force me in, slam the door closed, and lock it.

It actually wasn't as bad as I thought. The first time was a little scary, because everything is quiet, and I forgot to ask how long I was going to be there. It wasn't too long, maybe a minute. We filmed it from three different angles, so it took all day! Just before lunch, I was in The Chokey, and the door was locked. I heard Danny DeVito say, "Time for lunch everyone, let's go!" I shouted as loud as I could, "Don't forget me!" He was teasing, but for a moment, I thought he was going to leave me there!

I have a lot of fun with Danny. Last week, he was pretending to hit me across the face, and teaching me how to fall back. When visitors come to the set, we do it, just to shock them. It's my birthday tomorrow. I'm going to be eight.

MARA'S BIRTHDAY

I always wake up early on my birthday. My family gave me books and some games and a stuffed bear. I didn't really want to go to work. I just wanted to <u>play</u> all day. I thought that maybe nobody would know it was my birthday. Boy, was I wrong!

MY TRAILER WAS COVERED WITH BALLOONS, MAYBE **FIVE HUNDRED** OF THEM!

Inside my trailer were lots of presents from the DeVitos and all the people I work with. My mom told me I was going to be spoiled!

We worked all morning, and at lunchtime I got a huge chocolate cake, with red frosting in the shape of Matilda's big red ribbon. Everyone I work with sang **"Happy Birthday"** to me.

This weekend, I am having a party at the doll museum with my friends from school. I can't wait. I miss them.

PROPS

DANNY DeVITO has taken extra care to make this movie SPECIAL—little things, that only we know about.

When we first started filming, Danny told me that he wanted Matilda to have a doll, and asked me to design it.

He told me, "Think wild, and create a doll from the scraps that Zinnia would have thrown away." It was a cool project. I went home and made a drawing of a rag doll. Danny loved it, and Wanda was made into a REAL RAG DOLL. (I helped sew her together too.)

wears Mrs. Wormwood's make-up

wears nail polish

has clip from magazines

ROALD DAHL, the author of <u>Matilda</u>, died in 1990, but Danny sneaked some of his things into the movie as props. His walking stick and coat were used in Magnus's house. (That's Miss Honey's father.) Matilda was reading <u>Charlie and the Chocolate Factory</u> in the library scene.

The portrait of Magnus was even painted from a photograph of Mr. Dahl when he was in the Royal Air Force.

A photograph of him was on the table in Miss Honey's house.

The portrait of Miss Honey as a baby was painted from a photograph of my little sister, Anna.

ADOPTION DAY

Today we are filming Matilda's adoption.
I LOVE WORKING WITH RHEA PERLMAN.

I don't know how I keep from cracking up, because she is so funny! This morning, when I saw Zinnia with her wild clothes and crazy hair, I thought, <u>Oh gosh, I'm going to spend the day laughing</u>. She tells me silly stories. My favorite is the one about her hamster, who likes to go skiing in Wyoming. He wears ski boots, a parka, and goggles. He doesn't like white-water rafting, but he does like to surf.

THE FINAL WEEK

It is Monday. <u>This is our last week of filming</u>. Everyone is a little sad . . . including me.

There are four main steps to making a film:

THE SCRIPT.   THE CASTING.
THE FILMING.   THE EDITING.

Now the first three parts are complete. DANNY DeVITO, the producers, and the editors will continue working every day, but the actors and crew will move on to other things. I will go back to school.

When the filming part is complete, it is called a <u>W R A P</u>. Then comes the wrap party! It is going to be at the flying museum. There will be dancing and food, a kids' fairground, a flight simulator, and games. All of us will be together again one last time.

I hope my mom lets me stay up <u>late!</u>

We filmed the last scene today.
We were all supposed to be HAPPY!
We acted well, but really I was a little SAD.
I don't like saying good-bye.

I will miss all my new friends.
But I will never, ever forget them.